A Walk in the
Rain

written by Rosemary Border
illustrated by Pauline King

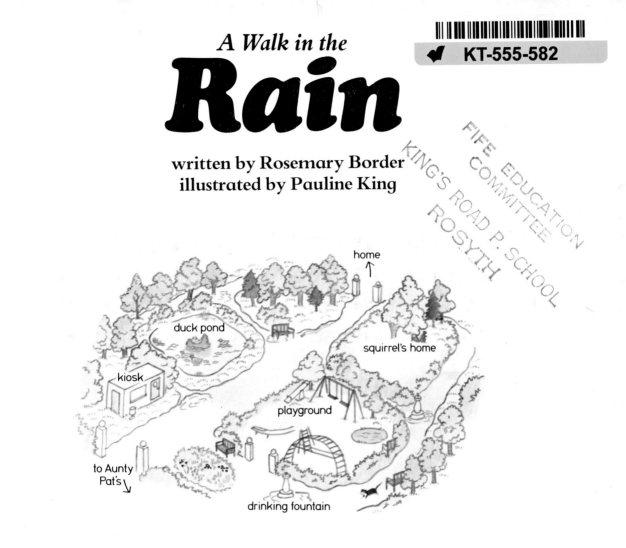

home

duck pond

squirrel's home

kiosk

playground

to Aunty
Pat's

drinking fountain

Macdonald 345

David and Jessica and their dog Silky often cross the park to visit Aunty Pat. Mummy telephones first, then she takes them to the park gates. Aunty Pat waits at the other side of the park. She can see them every inch of the way! All the same, it is an exciting adventure for them, even when the weather is cold and rainy.

David looked like a lifeboatman in his shiny yellow mackintosh, hat and boots. Jessica wore her new splash suit with all the zips. The rain fell in fat, shining drops into the black puddles. Each drop made a ring that spread and spread. More raindrops hung in neat rows along the underside of the railings. In the distance the children could hear the cars splashing along the wet street. In the park everything was quiet except for the birds twittering and the plip-plop of the rain.

The gully at the side of the path was now a fast little stream. David put a stick in the water. It floated down the stream and gurgled down the iron grating. Silky watched. She wished she could chase it. The park keeper's cat sheltered under a bench. It hated the rain. Silky growled and pulled on her lead. *She* didn't mind the rain. One shake of her dense, thick coat and she would be quite dry again.

David spotted a big puddle and yelled 'Come on!' He jumped in it with both feet. Jessica squealed and laughed as the muddy water splashed everywhere. The next puddle was all the colours of the rainbow. 'That's oil,' said David, 'from the park keeper's lawnmower, I expect.' Jessica stirred the water with a stick. The rainbows made a swirly pattern. 'Pretty,' said Jessica.

They passed the duckpond with its green island in the middle. The ducks were enjoying the rain and were swimming about busily. Each left a frilly wake in the water like a boat. They saw the children and swam towards them. 'No bread today. Sorry, ducks,' said David. 'Sorry ducks,' said Jessica. Silky barked and pulled. She wanted to chase the ducks.

The sandpit in the playground was a wet brown colour instead of its usual pale gold. It was pitted with little holes that the raindrops had made. There was a big pool of water on the ground at the foot of the slide. In the dip of the wet, silvery slide was another, smaller pool.

'You'll get a wet bottom if you slide today,' David told Jessica.

A lady sat on a bench near the playground. She had a paper carrier bag, and the rain had made it soggy. She was grumpily taking her shopping out of the paper carrier and putting it into a plastic one. 'Plastic is waterproof,' explained David to Jessica. 'The water can't get through. Like my mac.' 'Is my suit waterproof?' asked Jessica. David did not know.

They saw Aunty Pat waving. Jessica let go of David's hand and ran to meet her. Then – splat! Down she went, flat on her face in a puddle. David let go of Silky and rushed to help his sister. Silky saw the park keeper's cat on the climbing frame and she was off! It was all over in a moment. Aunty Pat picked Jessica up and dried her face. David caught Silky and smacked her. The cat growled and spat from the top of the climbing frame.

Jessica was not hurt at all, and her splash suit had kept her quite dry. Suddenly she had an idea. She ran to the slide. 'Whee!' she shouted as she shot down. Splash! she hit the bottom. Water flew everywhere. With a big grin Jessica ran back to the others. 'Waterproof,' she said.